THE SANTA SEASON

LINDA FORD

AN
APPLE
PAPERBACK

SCHOLASTIC INC.

New York Toronto London Auckland Sydney
Mexico City New Delhi Hong Kong Buenos Aires

*To Amy and Kristin at Scholastic —
you've been great.*

If you like this book, look for these other Apple Paperbacks
by Linda Ford:

Santa Claus, Inc.
Santa S.O.S.
The Santa Solution
The Santa Contest

ISBN 0-439-43532-3

12 11 10 9 8 7 6 5 4 3 2 1   2 3 4 5 6 7/0

Printed in the U.S.A.   40

First printing, December 2002

CHAPTER 1

I guess I should have left it up at the North Pole. But it seemed like such a cool idea — I had to bring it home with me. I remember thinking that it couldn't hurt to just *look* at it.

That was my first mistake. *Thinking*.

Of course, I didn't know what it was, not for sure. But it had to be something pretty amazing.

"I think it's a time machine," April had said.

Personally, I thought it looked more like a vacuum cleaner. But I'd rather have a time machine any day.

I'd spent a lot of time at the North Pole that January, hiding in my great-great-great-great-grandfather's workshop. Yeah, I mean hiding. I hadn't wanted to be at the North Pole in the first place; it isn't my favorite spot in the world. But I had to change my plans when some obnoxious relatives showed up on our doorstep. Those relatives were Cousin Buck and his son, Rammer, and April, Rammer's mom. And when I said they were *obnoxious*, I was being *nice* about it. I mean, what can you say about a kid who glues your grandfather's pants to his seat?

Truthfully, April wasn't so bad — the humiliating part is that Buck and Rammer are the ones who are actually related to us. April just married into the family.

"They're cousins," Dad says, "*several* times removed."

Buck had tracked us down because he wanted to meet the Santa Claus branch of the family. You see, my granddad is the current Santa and when he retires my dad will be Santa and then . . . well, I was supposed to be next. But I'm allergic to reindeer, and they really don't like me, and I get airsick in the sleigh, and . . . well, I have a long list of reasons why I shouldn't be Santa and it's kind of embarrassing. Mostly I just don't *want* to be Santa Claus and my twin sister does, so that's how we worked it out. Granddad and Dad decided that Marcia would inherit the family business and grow up to wear the big red suit.

But we hit a snag when Buck thought Rammer

ought to get a chance to try out for the Santa job. That's how I ended up at the North Pole again. I had to win a contest so I could name Marcia as Santa. While Rammer went through apprenticeship training, I holed up in the workshop so I didn't have to spend time with Buck.

Cousin April spent a lot of time with me in the workshop and we played around with some of the gadgets that no one had looked at in a hundred years. April is smart. She probably should have been an engineer. She was the one who figured out how to put this gadget together. She's smart enough that she probably would not have let me bring the time machine home.

Of course, my ancestor was the real genius. I mean, if he'd only invented the anti-gravity sleigh, he'd class up there with Einstein. Santa's sleigh flies, swoops, glides, hovers, whatever you need it to do. It's not magic — it's science.

"What did Santa Claus use on Christmas Eve *before* the anti-grav sleigh?" I once asked my dad.

"I never really thought about it," Dad said, looking puzzled. "He had to cover quite a bit of ground . . . it must have been easier after the new sleigh was invented."

It was just another mystery surrounding my genius ancestor. It's hard to believe all the stories about him.

He thought up a bunch of stuff that only science-fiction writers talk about. There's the M*E*D*A*R (Matter Energy Disassemble and Reassemble system) that transports Santa in and out of houses; it's kind of like being beamed up on *Star Trek*. Santa still uses the chimney once in a while, but the M*E*D*A*R is faster. We have a communication system that works like a telephone but doesn't need any wires. It's kind of like a cell phone, but we've had it for over a hundred years. The North Pole power plant is amazing, too. It runs the heat and lights and other machines, but it won't work anyplace except there (it has something to do with the gravitational pull), so it wouldn't do the power companies any good.

Even though my ancestor invented a ton of gadgets to make it easier for Santa to do his job, I didn't expect the machine I'd taken to work, not really. Great-great-great-great-grandpa left lots of unfinished projects around the workshop. I figured the time machine was one of his duds. My teacher says that's how science advances.

"We learn almost as much from our failures as from our successes," Mrs. Lopez always says to us when we screw up.

"Oh, sure. That's why there are so many statues for the losers," I told her.

"Every monument to success stands in the shadow of previous failures," said Mrs. Lopez, and then she grinned. "Besides, there are more failures than successes and who needs that many statues around?"

Mrs. Lopez is a pretty cool teacher and I wish I could show her my ancestor's invention. But security has to be pretty tight on everything connected with the family business. Not even my best friends know about it. Santa Claus, Inc., is a secret.

Oh well. I thought I could still have fun trying to figure out the gadget on my own. But it had been in my room for two months, and I'd gotten *no*where. It was really too bad that some of my great-great-great-great-grandfather's genius hadn't passed down to me.

I was messing with the machine one Friday evening. It was sitting on my window seat, and I was trying to double-check whether everything was connected like it was supposed to be. I threw a blanket over it when I heard Marcia knocking. She always taps three times and then waits and knocks again twice. It's kind of our secret code. So far none of our little sisters have caught on.

"So what's up?" Marcia said as she stepped into the room.

"Just trying to think of how we can get out of cleaning the garage tomorrow."

"You know, if you hadn't hit the baseball through the garage window, Mom wouldn't be making us do it."

"Great. It's a little late to tell me that now."

"I would have told you before, but I didn't know you'd hit that pitch foul. So tell me what's really going on and what's that?" Marcia asked. She pointed at the blanket.

"Junk." I knew Marcia would think the time machine was a bad idea, so I tried to avoid the topic.

"Yeah, and that thing reflecting in the window is your science project?"

Marcia was right. I realized that the blanket covered up the front, but the window was almost as clear as a mirror. She could see everything.

"It's nothing," I told her, and twitched the blanket to cover it completely.

"Come on, Nick," she said, and glared at me. "Don't treat me like some dumb geek who doesn't know the difference. I can recognize Santa Genius when I see it."

"Santa Genius?"

"I don't like saying great-great-great-great-grandpa. It's a pain keeping track of how many greats there are, so I call him Santa Genius."

"I guess that makes sense."

"So what is it?"

"April thought it was a time machine."

"And you are willing to trust the intellect of the woman who willingly married Buck Claus?"

"Everyone is entitled to a few mistakes." I defended April, even though I had to admit that Marcia had a point. Marrying Cousin Buck was a heck of a mistake.

"So what makes you think she's right and that this isn't a new generation of anti-grav?"

I made a face. "I don't know what it is, but I'd like to find out."

"Sounds dangerous to me. Did Santa Genius leave any instructions?"

"Not to work the thing. But he had plans for putting it together."

I pulled the machine out from under the blanket and set it on the bed so she could see. Marcia compared it against the blueprints. It did look kind of like a vacuum cleaner with a long oval body and tubes and switches. There weren't any electric cords, so I didn't know how it was powered.

"You know what I can't figure out?" I said after a while.

"Huh?"

"Why our genius ancestor didn't go into business as an inventor. With anti-gravity flight he could have made trains out-of-date before they even finished putting tracks across the country."

"Are you kidding? Back then he'd probably have been burned as a witch or something."

"Nah, they hadn't burned witches since Salem. That was way back in the sixteen hundreds, a long time before he was alive."

"Doesn't matter," Marcia said. "This stuff *still* looks like magic. It would have driven people crazy back in the eighteen hundreds. Those people were *primitive*. They didn't even have running water."

"Then how'd he think of stuff like this?"

"Genius, like Leonardo da Vinci dreaming up flying machines."

"Yeah," I agreed. "He must have been pretty amazing. You know, if this thing really was a time machine we could go back and ask him about it."

"Who, Da Vinci or Santa Genius?"

"I'm not choosy. How about checking in with them both?" I asked, thinking how great it would be. "If I could get it to work, maybe I could go back and see the 1928 Yankees and get their autographs and . . ."

Marcia sat up and stared at me. "You aren't really thinking of trying this thing out?"

"And you don't really think this thing works, do you?" I shrugged and felt embarrassed. "This thing can't possibly work, never in a million years, not if we prodded and pushed and pulled. It's a dud. It has to be."

"He was a genius. But who knows what works and what doesn't? For all you know it could half work and only send your head back in time."

I swallowed. She had a point. I knew how dangerous it could be, and I'm not a genius like our ancestor was.

"It can't work," I protested, hating to admit she was right — that it might work.

"He invented the time-slip."

I'd never thought of that. The time-slip device on the sleigh actually works like a limited time machine. When Santa Claus flies west over the international date line, for that part of the world it's already the next day. So the time-slip moves Santa back one day. Otherwise he wouldn't get to part of the world until the day after Christmas. It's a weird feeling. I had to fly the sleigh last Christmas, and when I got to the international date line, I pressed the button and *kerflash!* I went back in time one day — it made me dizzy for a couple of seconds, but that was it. Now I was feeling dizzy at the prospect that the vacuum cleaner could be a full-fledged time machine. If Santa Genius invented the time-slip, he could have mastered the real thing.

I groaned at Marcia. "Okay, you win. If this thing works, it isn't safe to have it here. How do I get it back to the North Pole without Granddad finding out and having a fit? You know this technology stuff makes him nervous. He doesn't even like computers." Obviously, our granddad didn't get any of the family genius, either.

"I'm going up there for spring break. It can go in a box of my stuff and Granddad doesn't have to know."

I hated to give up my toy. But I figured I'd already gotten into enough scrapes without the help of a time machine.

"Let's put it in that cardboard box so no one sees it," I suggested, giving up the hope of getting Babe Ruth's autograph. We both started to lift it up.

I don't know exactly what happened then. Maybe we both grabbed something we shouldn't have. Or maybe it was just dumb bad luck, like I specialize in, but a blue light flashed and it suddenly felt like we were falling through the air.

Falling, falling, falling . . . and me with no airsick bag handy!

CHAPTER
2

"What do you think you are doing, young man?" a sharp voice demanded.

"Huh?" I looked up and saw a woman standing over me with one hand on her hip and the other holding a broom. She looked like a character out of a play, with a long dress and a bonnet. And she was hopping mad.

"Well?"

"What?"

"That's great, Nick," Marcia interrupted from a couple feet away. "That machine can't possibly work, never in a million years, not if we prodded and pushed and pulled. It's a dud. It just *has* to be a dud."

"Okay, so I was wrong."

"So what else is new?"

Marcia was sitting in dirt with her knees pulled up to her chin. Her jeans were dusty and her hair looked like she'd combed it backwards, but otherwise she wasn't hurt. At least great-great-great-great-grandpa's machine had sent our bodies along with our heads.

"Explain yourselves this instant!" the woman demanded, and she sounded madder than ever. Her face was getting red — she probably didn't like being ignored. Then suddenly she stopped and screeched. "You have sat on my egg basket!"

"I . . . did?" Then I realized that my rear end was feeling a little damp. And on either side of me was an oozing pool of gooey yellow.

"Yuck," I groaned, and tried to stand. Everywhere I put down my hands I got slimed with raw egg.

"You wretched boys think it's funny to come here and harass me?!" she yelled.

She started toward me, shaking her broom, and I didn't worry anymore about how much egg I got on my hands.

"Come on, Nick!" Marcia yelled. She lunged for the woman and waved her hands and stuck out her tongue and then dashed away. Marcia's antics distracted her and gave me enough time to get to my feet and head for the gate. I only got

12

one or two swipes of that broom across my backside, but it didn't hurt since she wasn't really going for damage. Marcia didn't bother with the gate. She just leaped straight over the picket fence and ran.

The woman followed us for about a hundred feet and then gave up. Marcia and I kept running till we were sure it was safe. We stopped under a tree and I started to sit.

"Stop!" Marcia yelled.

"I gotta rest."

"If you don't get some of that goop off your pants you'll be caked in dirt."

She was right. I took a stick and scraped off as much as possible, which wasn't much, then threw myself down. I was exhausted.

"I don't want to move for a year."

"Speaking of years," Marcia said, "which one do you think this is?"

"Don't ask me. I didn't see any dates on that thing."

"Great."

If it weren't for all the weird things that have happened to me for the past year, I'd probably have figured I was having a really strange dream. But ever since I found out about Santa Claus, Inc., my dreams aren't as strange as my real life.

"It looks like we're in some kind of old West-ern," I said, pointing to a wagon going by. A man was driving, with a girl about my age sitting next to him. The man had on some dark pants, with suspenders, high boots, and a straw hat. The girl was wearing a long dress with sleeves down to her wrists and a bonnet so big you could hardly see her face.

"I'm glad I'm dressed like me and not her in a getup like that," Marcia said. "Jeans make so much more sense. She's got to be hot with all those clothes on."

"We're going to have to go back there," I finally said.

"Where?"

"To that lady's yard to find the time machine that brought us here. How else will we get home?"

"Bad news, genius. It didn't bring us here, it *sent* us here."

"What?"

"The machine didn't come with us. I checked."

"You just missed it," I insisted. "We'll sneak back and look."

Marcia just rolled her eyes. "Okay, O Brilliant One, but if I'm right and you're wrong, what are we going to do?"

I ignored that, mostly because I didn't have a clue.

14

We rested for about fifteen minutes and then started back, trying to look like two normal kids fooling around. But people kept staring. The problem was that we *weren't* normal kids; we were Santa's grandchildren and had just landed in the biggest mess of our lives. And it didn't help that it was all my fault, a fact I'm sure Marcia will never let me forget. And from the looks of things, she might have the next sixty or seventy years to rub it in. Just what year *was* this? It looked like a pretty old place to me, but I'm no expert.

Now that I wasn't running, I had time to look around — and it didn't look good. There weren't any modern houses. The homes were spread out and most had barns next to them or sometimes behind them. There weren't any telephone poles or electric lines. No one had an antenna on top of their roof for television. Once in a while someone in a horse and buggy drove past us. The women and the girls were wearing long dresses and the men had suspenders on, the ones who weren't wearing overalls, and most of the men had beards and hats. Unless we'd been dropped into a living history museum, we'd landed in a different century than the one we'd been born in.

"Here it is," Marcia said after a while.

"Are you sure this is the one?" I asked.

"Yeah. I never forget a place where I've been chased by a broom."

We checked carefully before opening the gate and sneaking into the yard.

"Here's where we landed," I said, pointing at a mess of eggshells and drying goop. "That's disgusting."

"The seat of your pants is pretty disgusting, too," Marcia noted.

"Couldn't resist, could you?" I grumbled.

"Nick, only you could travel through time and end up in an egg basket. Just be glad you didn't land five feet to the right."

I eyed the pile of manure and decided she had a point.

"This must have been before our house was built," I said. "Or else we'd have been transported back into my room upstairs. And that's why we fell. We had been on the second floor."

"Since when did you become such an expert on time travel?"

"It's a time machine, not a transporter," I answered, ignoring her sarcasm. "It moves us through time, not to different places."

"How do you know it doesn't do both?" Marcia countered.

Marcia had a really annoying habit of being right. I *didn't* know what kind of machine it was.

"Come on," I said, "we'd better look around for the time machine before that woman gets her broom out again."

We hunted but couldn't find a thing from the twenty-first century.

It was on the way out when we heard a far-away screech — "I told you boys to remove yourselves. Just you scat and do not come back!"

We hurried off.

You boys. I thought about what the woman had said. "She thought you were a boy, Marcia," I teased. No matter how much trouble we were in, it felt good to laugh.

Marcia blushed and then shrugged. "I don't think girls wear jeans much in this day, and they all have longer hair and bonnets and ribbons and stuff like that."

"Yeah." I slumped against a tree, really tired. It seemed like the middle of the day here, but it had been close to bedtime back in our own time.

"I guess you're right about one thing," Marcia said after a couple of minutes.

That woke me up. It was nice to be right about something in a mess like this.

"What?"

"We probably are home, sort of. That house over there is the same one on the corner down the street from our place."

She was right. People said the guy who built that house was pretty strange and kept adding stuff like little towers and tiny porches. There couldn't be two like it in the world.

"This must be sometime in the 1880s," Marcia continued. "Mom once said that house wasn't much older than ours, and our house was built in 1891."

"Then I know what we should do," I told her after thinking for a few minutes.

"What's that?"

"We've got to find Santa Claus."

"Santa?" Marcia asked sleepily.

"Yeah. Our great-great-great-great-grandfather. The genius, remember?"

"Is he still alive now? Most of the stuff I hear about him is from back in the 1840s."

"If he isn't, then we'll just have to find his son, or grandson."

"Great. I can just see us trying to explain this one."

CHAPTER 3

At first I thought we had to look for people named Claus.

"No, it's Martin," Marcia said.

"I thought it was only, like, fifty or sixty years ago that we became Martins. I mean, wasn't it just our great-great-grandfather who decided to change our name from Claus, to protect the family business?"

"Nah. It goes back much further than that. Before 1800."

I figured I'd have to trust Marcia on those facts, since she'd done some genealogy. She's into that.

It didn't take long to find Martins in town. The problem was finding the *right* Martins. It had to

19

be Nicholas Martin because it's the family tradition for the Santa heir to get that name. We walked out to a place in the country that someone told us about. No luck. That guy couldn't have been our ancestor, not unless we're descendants of Neanderthals.

"Ain't got children," he growled when we asked about his family. "Don't want children, don't intend to ever have children."

"That's good news for the children," Marcia said under her breath.

The man's eyes nearly bulged out of his head. "Get off my land!" he yelled. "Or I'll have the sheriff on you."

"Maybe they haven't moved here, yet," Marcia grumbled as we dragged ourselves back into town from the place in the country.

"Dad says his family practically founded this town."

"Dad exaggerates, you know that. Besides, it was a long time ago."

"Well, maybe he's using a different name. Not Nicholas, I mean."

"Ugh!" Marcia groaned. "Don't tell me we have to check every Martin in town."

"If we have to. Besides, there aren't *that* many."

Over the next few hours we went to three different Martin houses. The problem was trying to

figure out if they were the people we were looking for — without asking the kinds of questions
that would make them think we were nuts. I'm
not sure what they did to people who they decided were crazy back then, and I didn't want to
find out. Another problem was that even if we
asked the right questions, and it was the right
family, they might not tell us the truth. Maybe
security didn't have to be as tight as in the modern era, but Santa Claus, Inc., was still a big secret. So we visited people and asked things about
their families and said we were looking for an old
friend of our grandfather's. That was almost true
anyway.

If I hadn't been so worried, it might have been
kind of interesting. There were horses and wag-
ons and people dressed in strange clothing. Marcia said it was like an old movie, but it was a
little grubbier than movies. I mean, you don't
smell the horse droppings or the pigpens at the
theater.

Of course, people thought *our* clothes were a
little strange too. One woman asked us if we
were wearing some highfalutin fashions from
back east, whatever that meant. Another man
looked at my sneakers and said he figured they
were some kind of boating shoe, but why on
earth was I wearing them off the water? They all

probably thought we were idiots since we didn't say much and just rushed off.

Finally there was only one Martin left and for once we lucked out. The man at the blacksmith shop said he knew Edward Martin, and since he was headed that way, he'd give us a ride. I was really grateful, until I found out how hard the back of a wagon can be and how much it jiggles and bounces. It was almost as bad as Santa's sleigh. If it hadn't been so long since I'd eaten, I probably would have had an accident. Of course Marcia didn't have any problems.

"I can't believe it," she said to me. "You get airsick in a *wagon*?"

"Airsick?" the man asked over his shoulder. "What kind of condition is that? It's not catching, is it?"

"No," I answered through gritted teeth. "And I'm not airsick . . . I'm . . . wagon sick, sort of."

The man just looked confused, which was all right with me. "Nice going, Marcia," I muttered.

"Here it is," the man announced a few minutes later. We climbed down and looked around. "It's that house," the man said, and waved good-bye.

I couldn't believe it. We were back where we started! It wasn't possible. *That* house was the one where Attila the Hun lived . . . the one with a broom and five dozen smashed eggs.

I looked at Marcia. "Tell me he didn't point at that house."

"Well, he could have been pointing to the one next to it."

"Pleeeeeasssse let it be this one!" I moaned as we walked up the front walk of the other one.

We knocked and a man came to the door. "You kids need something?" he asked.

"We're looking for Edward Martin," I said politely. "Someone said he lives here."

"Edward?" He looked confused. "Don't know any Edward, but Nick Martin lives to the right of me."

"Nick?" Marcia asked eagerly. "You're sure it's Nick?"

"That's what he said the name was. They're fairly new. Just moved in from the country, I think."

"It's got to be the right one!" Marcia whispered triumphantly when the door was shut again. "His name is Nick! It makes sense. They probably built our house later, right next to their old one."

"You don't have to act so happy about it."

Her eyes opened and she made a face. "You're right. You don't suppose that woman is our . . . uh . . . great-great-something grandma. . . ."

"Don't say it! Don't even think it!"

* * *

We decided to postpone getting the bad news until the next day. By the time we'd gotten back to our starting point it was getting dark and I was so tired I could have slept on a cement slab. We were hungry, too, but there wasn't much we could do about that. So we found a barn where everything was quiet, crawled into the loft, and went to sleep on a pile of hay. In the morning a lady was really nice to us and fed us breakfast after we told her we were orphans and were looking for our grandparents.

"It's not really a lie," I whispered to Marcia when she scowled disapprovingly. "We *don't* have any parents here . . . only they're not dead, they just haven't been born yet."

After breakfast, we found a back way onto the Martin land and managed to sneak into their barn. I'm not sure what we were hoping to find. Proof, maybe, that we were related.

"No reindeer," Marcia whispered in disgust. "And not one piece of Santa Genius."

"He could hardly leave it around so everyone could see it, you know. He'd have to be careful."

"Well, what do we have here?" a voice said suddenly.

I jumped two feet in the air, expecting to meet a broom. Instead I saw an old man. He had white hair and a beard, with green eyes. Even if he was pretty old, he looked like he was strong enough to tackle a bull. But he didn't look mad to see us in his barn.

"We're . . . uh . . . looking for Nick . . . uh . . . Nicholas Martin," I managed to say with my dry throat."

"Who are you looking for, Nick or Nicholas?" the man asked with a grin.

"Does it make a difference?"

"Well, they're hardly interchangeable." He seemed to think it was a great joke.

"So what's the difference?" Marcia asked.

"Do you want the pompous one with the big head or the one who actually stands on his head?"

"Father!" a deep voice called and a second man stepped through the barn door. "Mabel wants to know if you're coming to breakfast." He was dressed in a suit and had long sideburns and a huge handlebar mustache. When he saw us he drew himself up stiffly. "Good heavens. You have caught them. Mabel told me about the two boys who terrorized her yesterday. Hold them here while I send for the sheriff."

"Don't be silly," the older man said, and his eyes twinkled. "These two fine young people are friends of mine."

The younger man's eyes narrowed. "Father. We

25

can't have hooligans running all over our property and you know that very well."

The white-haired man laughed. "Go to your store, Nicholas, and leave me to my friends."

"You know that I prefer to be called Edward."

Marcia's head whipped around and we stared silently at each other. So that was Edward, also known as Nicholas. That explained everyone's confusion with the names. Looking at Edward/Nicholas, I'd bet my next home run that he was the pompous one.

"Very well, Edward," his father said as though he were talking to a two-year-old having a tantrum. "Run along and get to your account books."

Edward made a bunch of huffing sounds before he marched out the door, a stuffy procession of one. His father turned back to study us. "Well, well," he said, "since we're such old friends, perhaps I should know your names."

"I'm Nick Mmmmah . . . , I'm Nick," I stuttered, pretty sure I shouldn't admit my last name was Martin.

"Nice to meet you, Nick-mah." He grinned and turned to Marcia. "And what's your name, young lady?"

Marcia's eyes shot open in shock. So far no one had thought she was anything except a boy, which wasn't so strange since girls did wear the *fussiest* clothes in the eighteen hundreds.

"I'm Marcia," my sister said quietly.

"Nice to meet you both. Anyone who can manage to terrorize Mabel and live to tell the tale must be interesting to know." He eyed my sneakers. "Hmmmm. Those look interesting as well."

I wasn't sure what to say. It was kind of weird. I'd been searching for someone like Granddad, who doesn't look at all like Santa until he puts on the red suit and his fake beard and stuff. This man looked exactly like Santa. Except for the fact that he wasn't wearing a red suit, he could have stepped right off a Christmas card. I don't know why, but just looking at him made me feel good.

Marcia asked, "Are you the one who stands on his head?"

The old guy threw back his head and laughed. "Under the right conditions, I certainly do."

I couldn't resist asking. "What conditions?"

"Oh, when I'm trying to invent new things, or figuring out how something works. The blood rushes into my head and helps me think of the most amazing possibilities."

"Then I think you're the one we want," I added.

"For what?"

Marcia nodded at me, so I took a deep breath and said, "Well, you're Santa Claus, aren't you?"

CHAPTER 4

The man's eyes opened slightly, but otherwise he didn't react. The air in the barn was still, and I'll always remember the dusty smell — mixed with some manure odor, of course.

"What makes you think something like that?" the man finally asked.

"We're . . . uh, pretty sure that Santa Claus moved here in the . . . um . . . well, a while back. I mean, Santa doesn't live at the North Pole all the time."

"Yeah," Marcia agreed. "Part of the time he lives like a normal person."

"Instead of like a legend?" he asked with a lifted eyebrow.

"Well, it isn't so bad up at the North Pole," I

said. "But it's a long way from the rest of the world and other people."

"And you think the company of elves might get tiresome?" he asked, as though it were a great joke.

"Oh, we know there aren't any elves," Marcia told him. "Just short Laplanders."

His eyes widened a little more at that.

"And I'll bet it's no trouble flying up there when you need to check on things," I added. "Or maybe you keep the sleigh at the North Pole and they come down to get you."

He chuckled. "Okay, you two, it's a fine joke. But I'm no Mabel. You can't get me going like you did my daughter-in-law."

The mention of Mabel made me shiver. For some reason I was completely sure that this man was my ancestor. I kind of liked the guy, but that made Attila the Mabel and the pompous Nicholas Edward our ancestors too. It reminded me of the day we were told that Buck Claus actually was a cousin. It was really depressing when we found out the same gene pool had produced us all. Some relatives should just stay unintroduced.

But none of that helped us now. It was time for direct action. We needed his help.

"Was it you," I asked, "or was it your father, who invented the anti-gravity sleigh? And the time-slip?"

"And the M*E*D*A*R system?" Marcia added.

His forehead wrinkled. "Just who are you?"

"It depends," I told him.

"On what?"

"On who *you* are."

"Then let's pretend that I did invent those fantastic things."

"Then we'd be your great-great-great-great-grandchildren." I counted it out on my fingers to make sure I got the right number of greats.

He stared at us for a couple of minutes and I started to wonder if he'd blown a circuit. I'd hate to see such a jolly man turn mad. Then his face lit up and it looked like firecrackers and sparks were shooting through his eyes.

"Good glory!" he exclaimed with a grin. "You must have found the time machine!"

* * *

There was a sort of awkward silence. It's not every day you meet your long-dead great-great-great-great-grandfather. And he was different than I'd thought he would be. I'd pictured someone sort of like a skinny little Albert Einstein, with horn-rimmed glasses, who spent all his time in a laboratory, nothing like this giddy old guy. He suddenly reached out and grabbed us both in a hug off the ground.

"It's a pleasure," he said, putting us down.

"We've been looking all over for you," I gasped. "We need help. We didn't mean to go traveling in time and we don't know how to get home. Can you use the time machine to send us back?"

"Hmmm." He rubbed his cheek and fluffed up his beard and wrinkled his forehead. "I would, but I haven't quite finished it yet. To be honest, I haven't been sure I'd be able to get it to work."

With terrific news like that I had a sinking feeling we might never get out of this mess.

"But it does, or else we wouldn't be here," said my sister, the optimist. "Will it take long to finish working on it?" Marcia asked.

"Oh, I don't know. Probably not, but I'd hate to test it for the first time on the two of you. Not to mention the fact that I left it up at the North Pole. We'll have to wait till the next sleigh run to get ahold of it."

"Can't you call them?" I asked.

"I'm afraid my voice isn't loud enough for that."

"No, I mean with the sub-atomic wave-particle something-or-other telephone . . . the special one, you know, that only calls the North Pole."

"Hmmmm," he said, and rubbed his nose. "I've been thinking about a design for a communication system to use in between sleigh runs. Something along the idea of Alexander Graham Bell's new telephone, but without wires . . . we can't run those between the North Pole and here. We don't even have Bell's telephone in town yet. You telling me I actually invent one?"

"You sure do," Marcia told him.

He grinned, white teeth against his bronze cheeks. "Well, I never," he said with a shake of his head. "That's terrific."

"Hey, Mr. Niiii-iiiick," a voice called from a ways off. "It's time for the game."

He jumped into the air and exclaimed, "Good glory, I forgot! Come on, you two, the game's about to start. I can't leave you here."

"Game?" I asked as he grabbed our hands and hurried us toward the barn door.

"But isn't there something we can do while we're waiting for the next sleigh?" Marcia huffed as he ran.

"There certainly is," he said. "We can play baseball!"

* * *

The next thing I knew we were rushing out onto the street. Grandpa Nick whistled and a red-haired boy with about a million freckles stepped out from the middle of a bush. He grinned.

"Still hiding from Mabel, I see," Grandpa Nick chuckled.

"I'm sorry, Mr. Nick, but that lady is scary."

"You're telling me, Jasper!" He winked. "That's why you've got to meet these grandchildren of mine. I hear they gave my daughter-in-law a jolly old fright yesterday and they still stand here today, alive and well."

Jasper turned admiring eyes on us. "No foolin'?"

"Well . . ." I hesitated, not wanting to brag, since I remembered Mabel had landed one or two strong swipes with the broom.

But Marcia didn't skip a beat. "We sure did," she told him. "And we didn't even know we were related to her at the time."

"Gosh-a-mighty!" he breathed.

"You go on and tell everyone I'm on my way," Grandpa Nick said, "and that we've got two more players for today's game."

Jasper let out a yell and sprinted down the street. Grandpa Nick turned to the front of the house and called, "Hezekiah! We're off to play some baseball. How about you join us for once?"

A boy about my age stepped out, dressed in the fussiest suit I've ever seen. It was dark blue and had lace on the collar and shirt cuffs. He had a sulky look in his eyes and his mouth looked like it was glued into a permanent pout. A fat little pug dog minced down the steps beside him.

"I don't play such rowdy games, Grandfather," the boy said, and his voice sounded as sulky as he looked. "And you know that Mother says I mustn't associate with those hooligans."

The old man shook his head. "You might have some fun, so if you change your mind, we'll be down the street." He walked a couple of steps, then turned back. "Oh, and tell your mother we'll have houseguests for a while."

The boy glared at Marcia and me before mincing up the steps again. The fat little pug dog imitated him, or maybe it was the other way around.

"Who is that?" I asked.

Grandpa Nick grinned down at me sympathetically. "Well, that might be your great-great-grandfather."

"That . . . that *nerd*?" I gasped.

"Nerd . . . ? Hmmm. Never heard that word before but it sounds like a pretty accurate description. Give him a chance, though. I think he's got potential."

Grandpa Nick was an optimist. But like I said before, I think some relatives should stay unintroduced.

CHAPTER 5

"All right, Nick, you can do it!" Marcia yelled from second base. She'd hit a double and if she got home we'd tie the game. If I got home we'd win it.

Not that winning or losing was a big deal to these teams. They just liked to play and Grandpa Nick liked to play with them. I'd thought he'd be the umpire or something, but he played along with everyone else and a little kid called Squinty made the calls for strikes and outs.

* * *

"This is my grandson Nick," Grandpa Nick had introduced me when we arrived on the playing field, "and this is my granddaughter, Marcia."

"A girl?" one kid said. "Girls can't play base-ball."

"You're ouuuuuut," the others yelled.

"Mr. Nick's rules — everyone plays. If you don't agree, you can sit the game out."

"Fine, fine, she can play!" the kid exclaimed.

After that, Marcia was treated like everyone else, and no one dared ask why she was wearing pants instead of a dress. It was the most fun I'd ever had at a baseball game. I even managed not to worry about all the trouble we were in.

Well, I was a little worried about meeting Grandma Mabel again. Jasper was right — she was scary. And it wasn't like we were on her good side. In fact, it didn't sound like Grandpa Nick was, either, only he didn't seem to worry about it. I had no idea how he was going to explain us.

In the bottom of the ninth, I hit a home run and everyone cheered, even the other team.

"Same time, tomorrow?" Jasper asked before we left.

"Absolutely," Grandpa Nick answered.

We started back and I asked him about Mabel and what story we were supposed to tell.

"I'm not sure she and Edward could understand time-travel," Grandpa Nick said, scratching his head. "I'll say you're Joshua's children. Josh is my younger son. He went off to explore Africa years ago and we don't hear from him too often. Mabel likely doesn't think much of him, in any case. She grew up on the farm next to ours and they never got along well."

"What happens if they ask us what Africa is like?"

"They won't. I'm afraid this branch of the family doesn't have much intellectual curiosity."

"Grandpa Nick?" Marcia asked. "How come your son . . . uh . . . our great-great-great-grandfather . . . how come he wants you to call him Edward?"

"Well, that's his middle name, but we always called him Nick, or Nick Junior. Now he's decided he wants to be Nicholas Edward, with the emphasis on Edward. He says he's tired of people getting him mixed up with me and he also thinks it'll be good for business."

"Santa Claus, Inc.?"

"Nope, the mercantile business. He and Mabel have just started a store with Mabel's father. They sell a little of everything, nails, flour, fabric, pickles. I don't think he's very interested in inheriting the family business."

Wow. That was a shock. The way my family talked, every eldest son in the history of the Martin-Claus family couldn't wait to be Santa

. . . until me, of course. I wasn't sure what Grandpa Nick was going to think about my future career plans, either.

But then again, I was a little fuzzy about family history. Maybe Grandpa Nick's other son took over and called himself Nicholas. That would mean Attila the Mabel and Pompous Nicholas *weren't* our ancestors. I wouldn't mind finding out my great-great-great-grandfather had been the African explorer — that sounded pretty cool. I didn't say anything, but if . . . *when* I got back, I was going to check it out.

* * *

"Oh my, it is those hooligans!" Mabel screeched as soon as she saw us. "That boy," she said, pointing at Marcia, "he attacked me, and the other one sat on my egg basket!"

"Ohhhhhh." Grandpa Nick squinted and looked me up and down. "So that explains your backside."

I made a face. The seat of my pants was stiff as cardboard from the dried egg and dirt. I just hoped it didn't smell.

"Well, perhaps you could wash his britches, seeing how it was your eggs that made such a mess of them," Grandpa Nick suggested. Mabel's face turned purple. Marcia smothered a giggle. "In the meantime I want you to meet some long-lost family. These are Josh's children."

"Josh Martin's children?" Mabel asked sharply. "I didn't know he had any."

"Well, apparently he does." She narrowed her eyes at that, but Grandpa Nick blandly ignored her. "So they're staying with me for a while and since you're staying too until the new house is built, we'll be quite a family in the place."

Marcia and I looked at each other and half smiled. So it was Grandpa Nick's house and he was in charge. Finally, some good news.

"What are they called?" Mabel asked grudgingly.

"This here's Nick." Grandpa Nick beamed. "So nice to have another Nicholas in the family."

Mabel drew herself up stiffly. "You know very well that we named Hezekiah for my father and of course Nicholas is his second name, for the Martin tradition."

"Well, of course, Mabel. What's wrong with that? Especially as dear little Hezekiah is the spitting image of his namesake."

I figured Mabel would pitch a fit, but she didn't seem to understand sarcasm. She beamed and nodded.

"Yes," she said, "so many people have remarked on the likeness."

"Yep," Grandpa agreed, "Hezekiah Junior is really a chip off the old block." I had a sudden image of an old man in a fussy suit mincing up the steps next to a pug dog. Good grief! If Hezekiah turned out to be my great-great-grandfather, then that old man would be *my* ancestor, too. I was ready to die of embarrassment, but Mabel seemed to think it was a compliment.

In a slightly better humor, she turned to Marcia. "My goodness, boy, you need a haircut. What is your name?"

"Marcia," my sister said with a grin.

"Marcia? But isn't that more of a . . . a . . . girl's name? Oh dear, you poor boy. How could Josh do something like that? He was always so eccentric."

"Not that eccentric, Mabel," Grandpa Nick told her, "since Marcia is a fine young lady."

Mabel drew herself up like a cat ready to spit at a dog. "A girl? With her hair cut like that and dressed in that disgraceful fashion?"

"What's disgraceful about it? Seems quite sensible to me, and she'd have a hard time playing good baseball in a skirt."

"Baseball? What on earth? That child is completely corrupted and *you* are not going to set her straight! It'll be up to me and oh, such a task it will be."

"You won't set her anything," he said. "Marcia can dress however she likes while she's staying with me, and we're definitely not going to lose a great outfielder for your notions."

Mabel snapped her lips together so tight they almost disappeared. "I feel sorry for that poor child, I truly do. You'll ruin her with your fool ideas."

"I will certainly do my best."

She drew her long skirt around her and her lips kept jerking like she wanted to say something but couldn't decide what. Finally she marched around the side of the house. But Grandpa Nick wasn't finished yet.

"Women should get the vote," he called, "even you, Mabel!" Her back jerked, but otherwise she didn't stop.

Marcia collapsed on the ground in a fit of giggles. I was in awe. Mabel didn't phase the old man, not for a second.

"That was amazing!" I said.

"It sure was," Marcia gasped, "but couldn't all the women get the vote, *except* Mabel?"

"Now, now." He wagged a finger at her. "Fair is fair. By the way, women do get the vote someday, don't they?"

"Yeah," Marcia agreed. "I think it was sometime around 1920."

"Not till then?" He frowned.

I nudged Marcia. "Maybe we shouldn't tell him

about what happens in the future. Isn't that, like, against time-travel rules?"

"Uh . . . maybe."

Grandpa Nick's eyes sparkled. "Time-travel rules? Have they worked out an ethical philosophy for traveling in time?"

"Well, no," I told him. "I mean, no one's ever done it before. At least no one I know, except in books and things. But in shows like *Star Trek* they talk about how time travelers shouldn't let people know too much because it might interrupt the time line and change the way things were supposed to happen."

"What's *Star Trek*?"

"It's just science fiction."

"How can science be fiction?"

"It's what they call imaginary stuff . . . stories about living on other planets, or computers that think for themselves."

"What's a computer?" he demanded in great excitement.

"Give it up, Nick," Marcia advised. "We could spend the next twenty years explaining it."

Grandpa Nick sighed. "It sounds as though you live in an amazing time."

"I guess so, but I can tell you this much. A lot of the stuff you've invented would *still* be considered science fiction where we come from!"

CHAPTER 6

"Safe!" Squinty yelled when Marcia slid into third base.

Every afternoon we played baseball. There wasn't anything else to do. We just had to wait. Since Santa Claus, Inc., didn't have the special telephone yet, the sleigh made regular trips from the North Pole to see if Santa Claus needed anything. Grandpa Nick said he wasn't expecting it for another week. It gave me time to worry.

I mean, who's to say how long Grandpa Nick would need to finish his machine? We might be stuck here for years. Spending time with Grandpa Nick was okay. But it would really mess with everyone's head in our own time period if we either disappeared and reappeared years later, or reappeared the same time we left but much older. It messed with *my* head just thinking about it. That was assuming the machine worked in the first place. Sure, since it worked once, you'd think it would work again, but experimental stuff is difficult to predict. Anyway, it was hard not to worry.

Grandpa Nick didn't worry. He pointed us to a trunk of old clothes and said to rummage around for whatever we wanted. Mabel washed my pants, grumbling the whole time. Marcia washed her own — she wanted to protect them from Mabel. For in-between times we found some funny, old-fashioned stuff in the trunk. Marcia even wore the dresses once in a while, but she preferred her jeans. I liked my clothes best, too, but you have to wear something while the other stuff is washed (by hand!) and then hung on a clothesline (no dryers in the 1880s).

There were plenty of things that weren't so cool about the 1880s. I think the worst was using the outhouse instead of a bathroom with modern plumbing. For anyone who doesn't know what it is, an outhouse is a tiny little building out in the yard, with a seat that has a hole in it, built over a deep pit where . . . well, you get the picture. My mom's parents have lots of doodads decorated with outhouses. They think they're cute. I don't know why; outhouses *smell* and they're not at all convenient in the middle of the night.

The other bad part was Edward, Mabel, and Hezekiah. Mabel didn't chase me with a broom anymore, but that didn't make her any fun to be around. She spent some of the time with Edward at the store, so we got a little relief. But Hezekiah was a pill and he watched us all the time as though we were crooks on parole and he was planning to report us or something. Grandpa Nick warned us not to say anything about Santa Claus, Inc., around him.

"Is he a pain about it?" Marcia asked.

"He probably would be, if he knew about it."

"He's as old as us, isn't he?"

"A bit older, but Mabel and Nicholas Edward have decided they want him to have a normal childhood and not be burdened with the family secret. In their minds, it is a burden. They don't plan to tell him until he's an adult."

"Oh."

I thought about it. Mom and Dad had waited till we were ten to tell us the truth, so we could have a normal childhood, too, at least for a while. Nothing had been very normal since then. I wonder if it would be better not to know. At least I wouldn't have spent so much time sneezing around reindeer or getting airsick in the sleigh. And it wasn't easy keeping a big secret like that from my best friends. But I could live with it, and knowing might even do Hezekiah some good. It might give him a different way of looking at things. It might make him less pouty and selfish. Even so, Grandpa Nick never gave up on him.

"How about it, Hezekiah? What about a game today?" he always asked.

Hezekiah didn't even respond. One day I got sick of him ignoring Grandpa Nick. And I was tired of him staring at me and saying nothing. I was out front waiting for Marcia before the game. He was sitting on the porch next to a decorated urn that Mabel thought was great art.

"Come on, Hez," I called, "we'll let you catch." And without thinking I tossed the ball toward the porch, but it wasn't headed for Hez — it was headed straight for Mabel's urn. I was going to be dead meat.

Hezekiah gasped. He lunged, his full body outstretched, and grabbed the ball a split second before it could crash into the big ugly vase. My jaw dropped open.

"Wow," I said, genuinely impressed. "That was some catch."

Hez just sat there and looked at the ball in his hands.

I thought he'd yell for his mother and tell on me. Instead he actually blushed and mumbled "Thanks" before tossing the ball back and disappearing into the house.

I told Marcia about it on the way to the field.

"He's that good?" she asked.

"At least that catch was."

Later I could have sworn I saw Hezekiah hiding behind a bush — watching the game.

* * *

The next day I knew I was right. Hezekiah was back in the bushes and watched each play from start to finish. So before the next ball game I snuck out and grabbed him.

"Keep your hands off me!" he snapped.

"We don't need spectators, but we do need a catcher. Come on!"

I half pulled, half pushed him up to the plate. "The position's all yours, unless you're scared."

"Am not!" he snarled.

"Good. Watch out for those fastballs."

The other members of my team were groaning. "That wet blanket will lose us the game," they murmured.

"Give him a chance," I insisted. "Remember, Mr. Nick says everyone gets to play."

That silenced them. Everyone did get to play, no matter what. I'd heard some of the neighbors grumbling because some black kids came and played with us and they liked it even less that some Irish kids from the other side of town were part of the team. It all sounded silly to me. What difference did it make? Grandpa Nick didn't care what the neighbors muttered about — everyone who wanted to play, did.

Hezekiah dropped the first rush to home plate, but after that he did pretty well. And when he came up to bat he whacked the ball so hard he just watched it flying up, up, up . . . until I suddenly realized he wasn't running the bases.

"Run!" I screamed at him, so he took off. By the time the other team had gotten the ball and was throwing it toward second he was rounding third base. "Stop there!" I screamed, but he didn't hear me and lunged for home. The other team's catcher was yelling for the ball. Then Hezekiah, the ball, and the catcher all seemed to get there at the same time and went tumbling over and over in the dirt.

"Safe! Safe! Safe!!!" Squinty screamed, and our team cheered.

Hezekiah wasn't injured, except for a small black eye, but his fancy suit would never be the same. He played the rest of the game covered with dirt and with his lace collar dangling down his back. But he didn't look too worried until we started home. When we got back, Mabel took one look at him and started screaming.

"Oh! Oh!!! My poor little boy. What have they done to you? I knew no good would come of having those hooligan cousins of yours around. We must get a doctor and, oh, they've destroyed your beautiful clothing. Oh my poor, hurt little boy!"

"Hurt, nothing," Grandpa Nick told her. "He just had a minor collision at home plate, nothing serious."

I don't know why he bothered saying anything. Mabel ignored him and glared at Marcia and me. My mom always uses the phrase "if looks could kill"; now I think I know what she means.

Of course, we thought that was the end of a great catcher, but the next day Hezekiah showed up in some old clothes I recognized from Grandpa Nick's trunk.

"Good going, Hez," I told him. "I never figured you could get your mother to let you play."

"She doesn't know," he whispered. "I've got to change back into my own clothes before she gets home from the store."

I wasn't sure what to say. Grandpa Nick wasn't an ordinary grown-up, that's for sure, but that didn't mean he'd help Hezekiah fool his mother. On the other hand, we didn't have to tell him that she didn't know. We never talked much about the games around "Aunt" Mabel and "Uncle" Edward, so maybe we'd get away with it.

So that's what we did. The next five days, Hezekiah sneaked into the barn to change his clothes while Marcia or I stood watch and the other one of us kept Grandpa Nick and Mabel busy. Then we did it again after the game. It wasn't too hard. Mabel was gone part of the time and mostly ignored us when she was there. Grandpa Nick spent a lot of time with paper and pencils working on some sort of plan. I hoped it was the time machine.

This was one mess we couldn't get out of by ourselves.

CHAPTER 7

The sleigh was due to arrive that night. Marcia and I sneaked out of the house and waited with Grandpa Nick. I didn't mind sneaking out on Mabel and Edward. They didn't know that Marcia and I knew about Santa Claus, Inc., and it seemed best not to clue them in. But I felt bad leaving Hezekiah out. He wasn't such a loser after all, especially when his parents weren't around. Even though I wanted to include him, I wasn't going to be the one to get in trouble for telling him about the family business. I had enough to worry about.

"They should arrive at half past midnight. They're usually right on time," Grandpa Nick said as we stood watching the northern sky.

Marcia yawned and looked barely awake. I probably didn't look any better. We'd been going to bed much earlier than in our own time. Since there weren't electric lights, or television or radio, or anything else, almost no one stayed up much past eight o'clock . . . and they got up by *five* in the morning! Marcia hated it and it was nearly killing me, since I'm more of a night owl. Tomorrow would be murder after such a late night. Tomorrow? It was already tomorrow.

I yawned until my teeth nearly fell out of my head. Grandpa Nick looked a little sleepy, but in a cheerful kind of way. He was pretty amazing. When I'd first seen him I'd thought he was really old because of his white hair. Now he seemed kind of young to me. Mom and Dad wouldn't think he was old. Heck, in my time he wouldn't even be retired yet. Marcia and I had always figured he was ancient back when he invented the anti-grav sleigh in the 1840s, and this was more than forty years later.

"You must be awful old by now," Marcia said through a yawn.

"It all depends," he answered.

"On what?" I asked.

"On how you look at it. I'm quite a bit older than the two of you, but compared to my son, I'm probably about your age."

Marcia and I laughed. "Uncle" Edward reminded me of the stingy old men who gave me a dime's tip for delivering flowers for my parents' flower shop and seemed to expect change back. He acted much older than Grandpa Nick or Granddad or even my mom's parents, who are kind of stuffy.

"It's just that it's been so long since you invented the sleigh," Marcia told him.

"Ohhhhh," he said. "Yep, that was forty-five years ago. But I was only twelve at the time."

"Twelve?" I gasped. It was hard to believe. I'd known he was a genius, but that was incredible.

"Well, I always liked gadgets and things of that sort. It was a Christmas present for my dad that year. Of course, I had to give it to him early, so he could practice for Christmas Eve."

"What did you use before that?" I asked.

"We had another system, but I figured I could come up with something that would be better. Something faster—and more fun."

"I wish we'd known you back then," Marcia said.

"Actually, I'm not much different now."

Now, *that* I could believe.

* * *

There was a whoosh and the sleigh set down in front of us. It hardly made a sound because the runners have anti-grav cushions for landing without snow. I hated that sleigh, I really did, but there was something fascinating about seeing something familiar from my time that was exactly the same in this one. But all I had to do was take one sniff of reindeer and I started to sneeze.

"Hi, Santa!" the man in the sleigh called. "Who are these visitors?"

"Good evening, Ludwig. These two are my grandchildren."

He nodded at us and turned to unload some packages. Marcia ran forward to get acquainted with the reindeer. I was staying as far away from them as possible. My allergy to the team was a good excuse, but the biggest reason was that I didn't want to find out if any of them disliked me as much as the modern-day Donner does—I've been kicked enough by reindeer!

"I need you to make another run tomorrow," Grandpa Nick told the man. "Here's a list of the things I'll need. Get Renny in the office to hunt up everything. Since he's helped me in the shop he'll know what I want."

"Sure thing, Santa," the man said, and tipped his straw hat. Yeah, it seems strange to think of someone driving Santa's sleigh in a straw hat, but it was June and he didn't need a warm hat till he got back toward the North Pole.

We helped carry the boxes into a locked room in the back of the barn, then stumbled off to bed. I couldn't believe how fast five A.M. came. The rest of the morning was sort of like sleep-walking until I crawled into the hayloft and took a nap. I barely woke up in time for the baseball game. Still, Marcia and I managed to wait with Grandpa Nick for the sleigh again that evening. It was the least we could do, seeing how he was the one who'd have to do all the work getting the time machine finished.

"Some of these things are fairly heavy," Grandpa Nick said. "Ludwig and I will carry them into the barn while you two keep track of the sleigh."

Marcia had woken up enough to visit with the reindeer again. "Hey, Nick," she said, "there's got to be a Donner in this team, just like in our time. I'd love to introduce the two of you."

"Very funny," I said, watching her. She knows I don't get along with reindeer—especially Donner. But wouldn't you know it? The reindeer loved my sister.

"Maybe nineteenth-century reindeer would like you," she suggested.

"Ha-ha."

"Wow!" The unexpected voice over my shoulder nearly scared me to death.

It was Hezekiah!

"Hez! What are you doing here?" I gasped.

"I thought maybe I was dreaming last night, but I wasn't. This contraption really is Santa's sleigh, is it not? And Grandfather is Santa Claus, right? That's what the man called him."

Marcia and I stared at each other. She made the face that means "we're in trouble now, and if anyone finds out I hope we can run fast enough."

"Do you think it's difficult to fly?" Hezekiah asked, and ran forward to climb into the sleigh.

"That isn't a very good idea," I warned. "It's a pretty complicated machine and flying isn't as easy as it seems. Believe me, it really isn't."

"So you've actually flown this thing?" he demanded.

"Well . . . yes, and it isn't a toy."

He picked up the reins.

"Stop it!" I hissed, and jumped in beside him to grab for the reins. The reindeer were getting restless. Marcia was trying to keep them calm. "Come on, Hez," I told him. "Get down, give me the reins, and we'll tell you all about it."

"Say!" Hezekiah exclaimed, ignoring me. "What are these for?"

"No!" I yelled, and tried to stop him.

I was too late. He punched the fast takeoff button.

Suddenly we were flying up, up, up!

And I *still* didn't have any airsick bags with me.

* * *

The jerk of the sleigh jolted me onto the floor and I banged my head on the seat, so I guess it wasn't the sleigh twirling the stars around. For a minute I closed my eyes tight and tried to keep my brain still. Over my head I could hear Hezekiah yelling "Giddyap!" to the reindeer. From the whistling of the wind I figured we were already going plenty fast.

"Stop telling them to go faster!" I finally managed to shout. "We've got to go back."

"Ah, don't be such a wet blanket," Hezekiah called back. "We're just going for a little ride."

Terrific. He was having a wonderful time and my stomach was already in revolt.

Somehow I managed to climb back onto the seat and fumble around for a seat belt . . . when I remembered that Granddad had only installed them a couple months ago . . . in *my* time.

"Hez," I tried to speak calmly. "We really need to go back. This isn't very safe, you know."

"What are you talking about? This is great!"

Then I realized we were flying steady and even. What do you know? Hezekiah was a natural, just like Marcia. But steady or not, my stomach didn't like it. Suddenly I couldn't hold it anymore and had to lunge for the side of the sleigh.

"I hope we're flying over a deserted field and you aren't dumping that on someone's front steps," Hezekiah cheerfully remarked.

"At the moment," I told him between clenched teeth, "I don't really care." I still wasn't sure whether Hezekiah was one of my ancestors, but right now he *really* reminded me of my sister.

"*They'll* care."

"Well, I don't see anything down there anyway."

"That's good."

Sitting back, I tried to think when the best time might be to snatch the reins out of Hezekiah's fingers without startling the team too much. These reindeer were strangers to me. How would they react if things got jerked around a bit? If Hezekiah would just hand them over, I could turn the sleigh around and find our way back to . . .

Another problem was wiggling around in the back of my head. Something else was wrong, but my head was spinning so much I couldn't think straight.

"How far do you think we've gone?" Hezekiah called through the whistling air.

"I've got no idea," I muttered. "It depends on

air speed and takeoff time and . . ." I suddenly stopped and leaned my head out to stare at the darkness below. Nothing was there, except once in a while a very faint glow from a window where someone still had a lantern lit.

I groaned. Now I knew what the problem was: I hadn't seen anything below. No malls, no electric lights, no freeways, no lighted billboards, none of the things that in my time were a sign of where we were. I didn't know what Grandpa Nick used for landmarks in *this* day and age.

How would we ever find our way home?

CHAPTER

8

"Is something wrong?" Hezekiah shouted. "Or are you just sick again?"

"Yeah, I'm sick. I'm really sick. I'm so sick I don't know if I'll ever get well again."

"Ah . . . it can't be that bad."

"Hez," I said through gritted teeth, "we have a problem. I don't know the way back to Grandpa Nick's place."

"Nothing to it," he answered. "We'll just turn around and fly in the opposite direction."

"It's not like we've been on a road, Hez," I tried to explain. "You don't know how many turns you've made or how fast you've gone. And even if you've gone in a straight line, even if you retrace your path exactly, you won't be able to tell when we're back home. Everything is just black. Hez, we're in trouble!"

"Don't be so scared. We'll figure it out," he said, and started to whistle.

I couldn't believe it. Two weeks ago I'd pegged Hezekiah as a number-one-class-A-nothing-but-a-pain-in-the-neck-*nerd*. Now he was acting like *I* was the one with the problem!

* * *

The sky was beginning to get light and we were absolutely lost. But this didn't bother Hezekiah.

"I guess we'll have to spend the day somewhere," he said. "And find our way back tonight. We probably shouldn't let anyone see us flying around in this thing."

"Glad to know you haven't completely lost your mind," I replied.

He landed in a wooded area, crawled into the backseat, and fell asleep. I wanted to do the same, but I hadn't gone through apprenticeship training for nothing. I pulled out the feed bags and gave the reindeer a meal, then started unhitching them, one by one.

"Nice reindeer," I muttered as one of them reared and snorted at me. I might have known—the name on its headband was *Donner*. This had to be my Donner's great-great-something-grandfather. "Take it easy!" I led him down to a creek I'd spotted. He snuffled in the water for a while and when he was finished I started back to the sleigh. That's when it happened.

It might have been an accident. The edge of the creek was muddy and he might have just slipped. All I know is that I saw a hoof headed for me and I ducked—and the only place to duck was into the creek. The nineteenth-century Donner scrambled up onto solid ground and stared down at me sitting in the water. Maybe it was my imagination, but I'm sure he was laughing. Now I knew exactly which reindeer ancestor had passed down such obnoxious genes to the Donner I know best.

"That's gratitude for you," I grumbled. "I should've let you go thirsty."

Lucky for me the water wasn't cold, so I only shivered a little, and I warmed up when I took the rest of the reindeer down for a drink. I didn't end up in the creek again, either, because I was smarter—or because they were nicer. Then I tethered them together so they could graze but not get very far.

The front seat of the sleigh was about as comfortable as sleeping on a rock, but I was so tired that I didn't care. My clothes were damp and clammy, so I pulled out a blanket from a side compartment, rolled up in it, and went to sleep. Or tried to sleep. Hezekiah snores. Every time I started to drift off he gave an especially loud snort. Finally I pulled the blanket up and wrapped the entire thing around my head—I only left space to breathe. That muffled the noise . . . a little.

* * *

I don't know what time it was when I woke up again. It was quiet, except for some birds, and I wanted to get back to sleep. And if I could have stopped my brain from worrying I might have been able to do it. But we were still in as much trouble now as we were before and I couldn't stop thinking about it.

Should we try to find someone around here? Someone who could tell us whether we needed to head north, south, east, or west to get to the right town. But we still wouldn't know when we got there, since we wouldn't recognize it at night. And there was always the possibility someone would ask questions about two boys out on their own and hand us over to the police. No, it was best not to get separated from the sleigh. So how were we supposed to find our way back? As if things weren't bad enough with Marcia and me stuck in the nineteenth century—now I had no idea how to find my way to Marcia and the time machine!

It was quiet so I knew I should try to get some more sleep.

Quiet. *Too* quiet.

I dragged myself up to check the backseat. No Hezekiah. Maybe he'd just gone into the woods for something. Twenty or thirty minutes must have gone by when I heard a faint noise. I listened as hard as I could.

"Help, Nick!" It was very soft, but that's what it sounded like, although it could have been my imagination.

Groaning, I climbed from the sleigh and headed in that direction. What kind of mess could he have gotten into? After five minutes it came again, louder this time.

"Hey, Nick, help!"

I broke into a run and crashed through bushes and trees. If anything happened to Hezekiah . . . well, I'm not sure what would happen to the time line. After all, *if* he's my great-great-grandfather and *if* something bad happened to him, would Marcia and I and everyone else I knew just blink out of existence? That's what the science fiction books and movies say.

"Ohhhhh!" I groaned. "Why didn't I leave that

time machine contraption back at the North Pole?"

"Help, Nick!"

"Hang on, Hez! I'm coming!" I practically screamed. "Where are you?"

"Here!"

Strangely, his voice was coming from above, so I looked up.

"Hi, Nick!" Hezekiah grinned down at me.

"You scared me!" I yelled. "I thought you were dying or in some kind of horrible danger!"

"Sorry. It's just that I've never climbed a tree before and I thought I'd like to give it a try. Only now I'm not sure how to get back down."

I stared at him. No, he probably hadn't climbed any trees before — even though there were tons of them in his backyard. Mabel likely kept him from doing *anything* interesting. Not that *I've* climbed very many trees, since I don't like getting high off the ground without a good floor under my feet. There was nothing I wanted to do less than climb that tree and help Hezekiah. But the future time line was at stake. Sure, if I winked out of existence I wouldn't have to explain myself to anyone, but that wasn't much consolation.

Somehow I managed to get up to where he was.

"Okay, Hez," I said through clenched teeth, and tried to keep my head from spinning. "Put your feet down where I tell you."

Slowly, we backed our way down the tree. About five feet from the ground Hezekiah got stuck.

"It's too far to reach," he objected.

"No it isn't," I insisted. "Just put your left foot there and your right foot down . . . no! your *right* foot!"

Almost like slow motion, I saw Hezekiah fall toward me. The next thing I knew I was lying on the ground, I couldn't see a thing, and my nose was in extreme pain. Hezekiah was sitting on my face.

I shoved and he moved.

"Thanks loads," I mumbled.

"Huh?"

"Are you hurt?"

"Nope."

"Good, because I'd like to strangle you!"

CHAPTER 9

Hezekiah didn't take my threat seriously. In fact, he was so cheerful it was downright nauseating.

"Have you figured out how we'll get home?" he asked.

"No!" I hissed.

We'd walked back to the sleigh and I was giving the reindeer some more grain from their feed bags.

"Ah-ah-choo!" The sneeze nearly took my head off. My eyes started watering, my nose was stuffed up, and I itched all over. Nineteenth-century reindeer were definitely just as bad for my allergies as the twenty-first-century variety.

"How do you usually find the way?" Hezekiah asked.

"Don't know," I mumbled. It wasn't as though I could explain about freeways and shopping centers and airports and other landmarks. He wouldn't believe me even if I did tell him, and I couldn't risk telling him the truth.

"What *do* you know?" he demanded.

"I . . ." I stopped and frowned.

There was one thing I *did* know how to find, even without any modern landmarks. We always use the stars to locate the North Pole. And there was probably someone up there who knew how to get back to Grandpa Nick's place. I heaved a sigh of relief and misery combined. It was going to mean a lot more time in the sleigh than I'd hoped.

"Okay," I told him, "I think I have a solution, but you've got to leave the controls alone and let me handle the sleigh."

"*I* want to fly!"

"Don't worry, you'll get plenty of flight time later on."

From the look on Hezekiah's face, I could tell there was no way he'd give up the chance to be Santa Claus someday. Which meant he probably did turn out to be my great-great-grandfather. Since I'd gotten to know him, that part didn't bother me quite as much, but I still wasn't thrilled about Attila the Mabel and pompous Uncle Edward, not to mention Hezekiah's namesake.

* * *

"My baby, my poor baby!" Mabel wailed and exclaimed over Hezekiah. She glared at me and then at Grandpa Nick. "That grandchild of yours nearly got my little boy killed!"

"Ah, Ma." Hezekiah twisted away from her. "It wasn't Nick's fault. He told me not to touch anything, but I wanted to fly it."

"My precious boy. You needn't try to protect that rowdy cousin of yours."

"Oh, Aunt Mabel, get a grip," Marcia told her. "I saw the whole thing, and it wasn't Nick's fault."

Mabel gave Marcia the most squinty-eyed scowl I'd ever seen. She looked like a cat ready to hiss. She had a habit of making that face. Hezekiah took the opportunity to jerk away from her clinging hands. "Hey, Grandpa Nick!" he exclaimed. "Will you give me some flying lessons?"

"Of course," the old man answered, "if your parents say it's all right."

Then Mabel's face just dropped. She looked so upset and scared, I kind of felt sorry for her.

"It's no use, Mabel. I'm sorry," Grandpa Nick told her, shaking his head. "But Hezekiah already knows the truth about Santa Claus, Inc., so there's no point in hiding it."

"Can I, Ma? Can I please learn to fly?" Hezekiah begged.

Her lips got tight, but I guess she knew she was licked. "Very well," she said stiffly. "As long as you're careful. I don't want you doing anything dangerous."

"Thanks, Ma! I'll be careful, I promise."

"In that case, Hezekiah," Grandpa Nick said, "how would you like to be Santa Claus someday?"

"Wow!" Hezekiah shouted. "You mean I don't have to sell nails and pickles?"

"Well, you'll have to do something until your father is ready to pass the job on to you. He'll be the next Santa Claus after I retire."

Hezekiah made a face. "You might as well skip him, Grandpa Nick. He *likes* selling pickles!"

* * *

I was happy that things turned out well, because I have to admit that the trip to the North Pole had been awful. It was freezing cold and we didn't have any jackets since it was summer back where we'd come from. We'd wrapped ourselves in every blanket we could find and I turned the seat warmers up as high as they would go, but I still felt like a Popsicle. My hands got so cold I could hardly feel the reins. I was hoping Hezekiah would believe that was why the sleigh flew so wobbly, except it started wobbling before it got cold.

"You should have let me fly," he said. "You don't do it so well."

"Just keep your feet braced under the foot rails," I answered.

It wasn't that I *wanted* to fly the stupid thing. Hezekiah was a natural, but he was still brandnew at it. If we had a problem, the two of us might get dumped out in midair before I could do anything to help.

"Ooops!" I gasped as the sleigh hit a downdraft and we dropped a sudden ten feet. Somehow I kept the sleigh steady and kept my stomach inside my stomach. Yes, I was a lousy pilot, but at least I'd logged hundreds of hours in the sleigh.

"Say, Nick," Hezekiah said, "how long have you been playing baseball?"

"About as long as I can remember," I said. Yeah, I thought, maybe it would be good to talk about something to get my mind off my stomach and everything else.

"Have you seen any of the big guys play?"

"Oh . . . once in a while we get to a stadium. That's a blast."

"Wish I could go sometime."

It was too bad. With Mabel and Edward as parents, Hez never did get a chance to do regular stuff like other kids. Now that he was loosening up, I kind of liked him.

"What's your favorite team?"

I tried to think of one that was playing in the 1800s. It couldn't be anyone from the American League, since it wasn't started till 1900, and I couldn't remember when the Cubs started or where the Giants and Dodgers were or . . . maybe it didn't matter. Hez didn't know the teams anyway. "Uh, the Yankees." I took a guess and then could have slapped myself. I remembered the Yankees were from the American League!

"Are they good?"

"Of course," I mumbled, so sick to my stomach I felt dizzy. "Only wish I could have seen the 1928 World Series and . . ." Good grief, I'd done it again.

"Huh? 1928!?"

"Did I say that? Boy, am I tired. I meant . . . 1878. They're, uh, just a small team from back east, but they're pretty good."

"You know? You don't look so good. Maybe I should fly."

"Okay . . . but just for a minute."

Hezekiah's mouth dropped open as we circled the North Pole complex. It was pretty impressive lying there in the middle of all that ice.

"Wow!" was all he could manage.

* * *

"Who are you?!" a man demanded when we'd landed in front of the largest barn.

I'd been so worried about getting home that I hadn't thought about the fact that *no one* in this time period knew who I was. Some other reindeer wranglers came running and surrounded us, like we were going to be arrested or something. What if they didn't believe us?

For a minute we all stood staring at one another. There probably hadn't ever been a situation like this at the North Pole. It's not like an army was needed to keep the place secret and safe, especially in the 1800s.

"We're, uh, Santa's grandchildren," I explained nervously. "We got lost and figured someone here might be able to take us back to his place down south." The way I stuttered, it's no wonder they looked suspicious.

"Oh really?" the first man asked.

"If it helps any, I remember that the guy who

73

came down the last two times was Ludwig, and I think Grandpa Nick said there was a man in the office named Renny."

The man examined me like a bug under a microscope.

I thought frantically. "Grandpa Nick . . . uh, plays baseball for the Reindeer team up here, and he said they won their last game!"

The other man grinned, and someone behind us called out, "Yeah, but we Snowballers will beat 'em in the rematch."

"Okay," the first man said, "we'll get you home."

"Could we get something warm to wear?" I asked.

"And something to eat!" Hezekiah added. "I'm starved."

Since they were standing around like they didn't know what to do next, I started toward the house, but Hez just stood there.

"Wow!" Hezekiah said as he looked at all of the buildings. He turned around in a circle to see everything. "What's that over there?" he demanded.

"It's one of the reindeer barns."

"And how about that?" He pointed to the top of a building with mostly windows and skylights.

"That's where the employees live."

"You mean real people work here? This is so incredible!"

A man tramped through the snow to us. "I'm Renny. Is one of you Hezekiah?" he asked.

"That's me!" Hez said, and shook the man's hand.

"You're a bit different than I thought you'd be," Renny said with a friendly grin.

"I guess I'm different than *I* thought I'd be too!" Hez agreed. "But I like the way I'm turning out."

"We'd better get inside and warm up," I suggested.

"Just let me know when you want to leave," Renny said.

It felt empty and lonely in the house. Grandpa Nick wasn't there, my real grandparents weren't even born yet, and Hezekiah didn't have anyone on this side of the family. Still, being there made me homesick. But maybe by the time we got back, Grandpa Nick would have the time machine finished. *If* he could get it to work . . . but I tried not to think about that.

I hunted around and found some clothes while Hezekiah scrounged around in the kitchen.

"You want some?" he asked, waving a weird-looking sandwich.

"Not a chance," I muttered. I was starving. But

who could enjoy food knowing it'd just be coming back the opposite direction it went down as soon as we got into the air?

We were flown home in style, wearing the strangest collection of old clothes I ever saw. When we got back to warmer weather we piled everything into the cargo space. I wished I'd kept the earmuffs on when I heard Mabel start yelling.

Marcia shook her head when I told her all about it.

"Grandpa Nick figured you'd head for the North Pole and be back tonight," she whispered when everything had settled down again. "That's what he told Mabel when she said that her poor baby must be smashed to pieces somewhere. He said the two of you were smart enough to take care of yourselves and the only problem was that we'd lost a first baseman and our catcher for a day. Then she got *really* mad and started screaming about him letting Hezekiah associate with those hooligans."

"I'll bet that was a show worth seeing," I whispered back.

"You haven't heard the best part." Marcia grinned. "After a while the sheriff came by to see what all the racket was about, and she yelled at him about her son going off in Santa's sleigh.

Then the sheriff told her he'd always thought she was crazy, and now he knew it for sure."

Mabel was glaring at us suspiciously, so I didn't crack so much as a smile. "What did old Attila say then?" I asked.

"She got so mad she couldn't say *anything*."

I just wish I had been there to see it.

CHAPTER 10

"You are never to fly again until you've gone through apprenticeship training," Grandpa Nick explained to Hezekiah. "You were lucky you didn't hit anything unusual."

"I did pretty good, though."

"He really did," I said. "Hezekiah's a natural."

We'd escaped the house, and Mabel's temper, and were hiding out in the barn loft. Grandpa Nick had brought up some sarsaparilla bottles and it wasn't bad, except I like twenty-first-century root beer better. Grandpa Nick said a guy named Charles Hires had started selling something called root beer, but he hadn't tasted it yet.

Hezekiah pointed at me. "Has *he* gone through apprenticeship training?"

Marcia choked on her sarsaparilla and sprayed some into the hay.

"Nice shot," I told her, hoping it would take Hezekiah's mind off my experience with Santa Claus, Inc.

"Well?" Hezekiah asked me. "Have you done apprenticeship?"

"Just for fun," I answered.

"*I* want to be Santa Claus someday!" he said firmly.

"Don't worry, you will," I said.

"Then why did you go through training?" he asked.

I shrugged. "Like I said, just for fun."

We couldn't tell Hezekiah that his job wasn't in danger from anyone who'd soon be traveling into another century. Grandpa Nick had said Hezekiah could probably handle the truth about time travel, but we still shouldn't tell him because he'd have to keep it a secret from his parents. Grandpa Nick didn't think that was fair to Mabel and Edward. He'd also said that if Hezekiah wanted to play baseball, his parents had to know about it. I think Mabel had screamed herself out, because she'd just glared when Hezekiah told her, and then she started pounding on something in the kitchen.

"You didn't look like you were having fun flying," Hezekiah said to me. "You kept sneezing and scratching yourself and the sleigh bobbed all over the place."

I blushed and avoided looking at Grandpa Nick.

Hezekiah looked sorry he'd joked about my flying ability, so he offered to get some more sarsaparilla. He really was turning out to be an okay guy. I was impressed that he hadn't blamed me for our unscheduled sleigh ride. Considering the way Mabel had been screaming, that took some courage.

"Is there something I should know?" Grandpa Nick asked, once Hezekiah was gone.

I might have guessed. Grandpa Nick was just about the smartest man in the history of the planet. He noticed *everything*.

Grandpa Nick leaned back and tugged on his white hair. "You don't have an older brother, do you?"

"No."

"And you have completed training, right?"

"Yes."

"And the sleigh wobbles and the reindeer make you sneeze and itch?"

"Yes, sir."

"Hmmmm. Tell me, Nick, do *you* want to be Santa Claus someday?"

Marcia hid her face in the hay while I turned red. "No, sir," I confessed. "I want to be an oceanographer."

"What's that?"

"I want to study the ocean and stop pollution and stuff like that." He looked confused, so I added quickly, "Pollution is a problem we've got in the twenty-first century."

"I see. So what about Santa Claus, Inc.? Do you have a younger brother who'd like the job?"

I knew I couldn't lie. "No, sir, just three little sisters. But actually, well, Marcia is really good at it and — "

"Marcia? Look at me, young lady."

My sister's face came up grinning. "Hope you don't mind too much, Grandpa Nick."

"It sounds like a perfectly logical plan to me. I just wish we could tell Mabel about it. That would really get her going!"

* * *

It seemed like forever waiting for Grandpa Nick to finish the time machine. I never saw it, but I'm pretty sure he was spending some time on his head, trying to get as much blood as possible flowing to help his thoughts. There was hay

81

in his hair once in a while — I hoped that was a good sign.

We were finally ready to give it a try.

"First we'll send a freshly laid egg and see how that works," Grandpa Nick suggested.

The next day the egg reappeared, cooked.

"Well, that isn't such a good idea," Grandpa Nick said.

I swallowed hard and agreed. He went back to tinkering on the machine for a few days. The next time the egg came back looking okay. Grandpa Nick put it back under the chicken to see if it would hatch. Then he sent a beetle. The beetle arrived whole and snapping mad. Later the egg hatched and the chick was perfectly normal.

"Now we can go home," Marcia said.

"I have a few more tests to make," Grandpa Nick told her. "And I've got to think it through completely. I'm not taking any chances on the two of you."

Thinking it through included plenty of baseball. We played every afternoon, and one day Grandpa Nick said he had a surprise. A man came by with a huge box thing on legs. The other kids got excited.

"Wow!" Squinty exclaimed. "I've always wanted one."

"What's that all about?" Marcia asked.

We were standing next to Grandpa Nick. Everyone else was talking to the strange man.

"Don't tell me they stop taking photographs in the future," he said.

"*That's* a camera?"

"Of course. Is it so different from later ones?"

"It's awful big. Most things in the future get a lot smaller."

"Hmmmm. Makes sense."

It sounded like he was already redesigning something. I sure hoped we weren't messing up the time line too much and that we'd recognize the future after we got back to it.

"I've done every test possible," Grandpa Nick told us three days later. "I can send you back anytime now, but we'll need to decide where to do it."

"I guess you can't send us back to Nick's room," Marcia commented.

"It doesn't exist now, so it would be difficult to get you into the right place. We need an open area so your reappearance won't collide with anything that's there in your own time zone."

"How about where we've been playing baseball?" I suggested. "It's a park now."

"Are there any trees in your century?"

"Some."

"Then we'd better find somewhere else. I don't want to take any chances. Of course, we could do it up at the North Pole. An ice field wouldn't have trees or buildings to interfere."

I shuddered. "Mom and Dad would have a fit if we disappeared and then phoned them from the North Pole."

"Aren't you planning to tell them about this little adventure?"

Marcia laughed. "I don't think they'll believe it. In fact, once we get back I think *we'll* have trouble believing it."

"That's understandable," Grandpa Nick told her. "But I'm still glad you came."

"How about the road in front of the house?" I asked. "If you send us back in the middle of the night there probably won't be any cars. It's a really quiet street."

"Right!" Marcia agreed. "And to be sure we don't get hit by a car, maybe we should climb up a ladder just above car level so we'll fall on a car if it's passing by."

"Cars," Grandpa Nick sighed. "I don't suppose you can explain those, either."

"Well," I answered, "let's just say that they're the kind of wagon we use back home."

"I would certainly love to see your century,"

Grandpa Nick said. "But I suppose it wouldn't be a good idea."

* * *

"I'm sorry to say that Nick and Marcia will have to be leaving us," Grandpa Nick announced at supper that night. "One last baseball game tomorrow and then later I'll put them on the night train back to their parents."

"Gee whiz," complained Hezekiah, "I wish you didn't have to go."

"Yes. Isn't that too bad," Mabel agreed, her face barely hiding her pleasure at the news. "I'll be sure to pack you some food to take along."

"Well, if you feel that bad about it," I said with a straight face, "maybe we could stay on a while longer."

"Oh. I'm sure your parents miss you too much for that," she answered quickly. "We can't be selfish in keeping you from them." Then she looked a little embarrassed, so I decided to let up on her.

"You'll . . . give your father our greetings, won't you?" Edward asked. "It's been a long time since I've seen him. Amazing thing, to go exploring like that."

His face looked almost wistful. It was the first crack in the pompous Edward that I'd seen so far. Of course, it would probably heal up right away, but it was nice to know he had a human side, especially since I was related to him.

"Why don't you come to our last game tomorrow?" I asked.

"Oh." He paused, and for a minute I thought he'd say yes. "I'd better not," he said. "I've got a shipment of pickles coming into the store tomorrow."

The last game was terrific. Hez made a lot of good catches and a couple of spectacular ones.

"Good one," Marcia even told him when he tagged her out.

"Gee, thanks," he said. "But it was just luck. If Jasper hadn't thrown it so fast, I'd never have been in time."

Yeah. I didn't mind being related to him.

* * *

"Isn't this terrific!" I muttered sarcastically as we hovered in the sleigh above the street. Grandpa Nick had decided it was the best way to raise us above car level. Even though the sleigh was holding steady, my stomach was not.

"I don't believe it," Marcia exclaimed. "We're only seven feet up and you're turning green as a pickle."

"You really weren't cut out for this, were you, Nick?" Grandpa Nick said. "Hope you don't get seasick, too."

"Nope, just in the air," I mumbled.

"Take care of yourselves," Grandpa Nick said after working the controls. I could see that the time machine had more parts than in our time zone. "I think we're set." He suddenly grabbed us both in a big bear hug. "It was nice to see a bit of the future."

Marcia wasn't embarrassed to cry and even I got a little choked up, although that was partly because I was airsick.

"I'm glad we came," Marcia said.

"Me, too," I managed to say. I didn't want to mess up the moment by losing my last meal over the side of the sleigh.

"When you're ready, you each grab hold and push that button," Grandpa Nick said. "But first, one last thing." He suddenly leaped over the side of the sleigh and yelled, "I think the occasion is right for this!"

And the last sight we had of the 1880s was Grandpa Nick — standing on his head.

CHAPTER 11

The second time we traveled through time wasn't nearly so bad as the first. At least we were prepared and we didn't fall as far. And I landed on my feet on the pavement, instead of on a bunch of raw eggs. Maybe my luck was improving — but I wasn't going to count on it.

"Do you think he got it right and this is the same night we left?" Marcia whispered.

"I hope so. We're going to have enough trouble getting back into the house." I had an idea about that and led the way to the backyard. The door was locked, so I knocked.

"Shouldn't we just sneak in?" Marcia hissed.

"Nick? Marcia?" Dad exclaimed when he

opened the door. "What on earth are you doing? You two are supposed to be in bed!"

"We were looking for Merry Christmas," I explained.

Merry and Christmas are my cat and dog. I know. It's really only half a name each, but they always travel in a pair.

"You don't think they've run away and found another home?" he asked, his voice just a little bit hopeful. He and Mom don't really want so many animals around.

Just then Merry Christmas came running out the door. Dad lifted an eyebrow.

"Why, imagine that," I said calmly. "And all this time I thought they were in the yard. They must have been hiding in the house."

"I smell a rat," Dad said.

"Well, don't show it to Merry Christmas," I told him. "They might want it for a pet."

With that Marcia and I trotted up to our rooms. I didn't think I was up to explaining where we'd been, and I *know* Mom and Dad weren't up for hearing it. It would just have to wait for another time.

* * *

We didn't get around to telling Mom and Dad about what happened. Maybe we should have, but we were back safe. Why worry them? It's not like we were going to try the machine again.

"We aren't, are we?" I asked Marcia one night.

"I don't think we should," she answered. "Grandpa Nick didn't say we couldn't, but you know he didn't leave all the parts on the machine. Those extra gadgets were the ones that told what times you could travel to. Maybe he thought it'd be safer if we left it alone. You know, sometimes I think it *was* all a dream."

"And we ended up having the same dream and sleepwalking in the yard?"

"That's what Mom and Dad would probably say."

* * *

The next afternoon I was alone at the house when the mail came. There was a big brownish-colored envelope in old-fashioned writing, addressed to Marcia and me. Believe it or not, the return address said: Hezekiah Nicholas Martin.

I should get a medal for waiting till Marcia got home to open it.

Dear Marcia and Nick:

I am leaving this letter with a law firm with instructions to mail it at the right time. When I was eighteen, Grandpa Nick told me about you and the time machine. He was quite a genius, wasn't he?

My father never became Santa Claus. He just kept selling nails and pickles and flour. That was okay because my baseball days were through by the time Grandpa Nick retired, and I was anxious to take over. I never was any great shakes as a ballplayer, but I did do a few professional seasons as a catcher. I'm better as Santa. After some practice I learned to do both a mobus and a Möbius in the sleigh. Pretty good, I think, for a kid who started out in a lace collar.

My grandson (your grandfather) is ten now, and he's quite a handful. Someday you should ask him about the time he flooded the largest reindeer barn so he could go ice-skating. What a mess!

Have fun.

From your great-great-grandfather, Hezekiah Nicholas Martin.

P.S. I left something for you under the northeast stone in the basement.

Marcia and I stared at each other for a split second and then raced each other for the basement.

The stone was stuck tight. I grabbed a crowbar.

"Mom and Dad aren't going to like it if you tear up the basement," Marcia warned.

"So, they can have our allowances to fix it."

I dug through the plaster filling the cracks

enough to pry up the stone. There was a metal box underneath!

Inside was another letter.

Dear Marcia and Nick:
Grandpa Nick asked me to find a way to get this to you. And I left you something else from me.
                                                    — Hez

There was a picture of all of us with Grandpa Nick at the baseball field.

"Pretty cool," I said.

"We look weird," Marcia answered. "We had to freeze so long for the camera we look like we're frozen stiff."

"At least we have it. Now you know it wasn't a dream. Hey, check this out."

I handed over a heavy round wad of paper with Marcia's name on it and took the one that had mine. Inside were baseballs, with *Babe Ruth's* autograph *and* the rest of the 1928 Yankees.

"Wow," I breathed. "I guess it really pays to meet your relatives."

"Don't forget, we might have gotten Hez, but we also got Mabel and Edward in the bargain."

That was true.

Of course, a lot of people would probably think Edward and Mabel were the nice respectable type of people we should be *proud* to have as ancestors, even if they were pompous and bad tempered. To some people Grandpa Nick would probably look like the oddball. But I was sure glad to meet him. He made all the Santa Claus stuff more amazing, like when I was a little kid and thought it was just magic. Now it was better than magic — it was Grandpa Nick.

After I thought about it, I did kind of admire Mabel and Edward. I can't understand them wanting to sell pickles and flour and things like that for a living. But if that's what they wanted to do, why not? Somebody has to. And they let Hez do what he really wanted in the end, even though they thought it was weird, and that's a good thing. I'm going to be an oceanographer, and they'd probably think that was weird, too.

So we're a weird family. I can live with it. I think. Besides, it's easy to put up with relatives who live in a different century — you're not as likely to run into them at a family reunion. Of course, with Santa Genius in the gene pool, you probably can't count on that.